BOO, BUNNY!

Kathryn O. Galbraith

Illustrated by Jeff Mack

sandpiper

HOUGHTON MIFFLIN HARCOURT

Boston New York

One shy bunny.
One dark night.

One hungry eye ...
two crooked teeth ...
one rattle of bones ...
two scaly feet!

One soft **whooooooo!**

One loud bOOOOO!

Jump.

Bump!

"Eeek!"

"Squeak!"

Hop-

hop-hop.

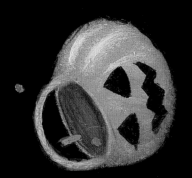

"Wait—stop!"

One bunny quivers.

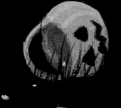

One bunny shivers.

One big door.
One hissing cat.

Two small bunnies

tap, tap, tap.

"Trick or treat,"
whispers one.

creak!

The door opens wide.

"Oh, thank you!"

Two giant hops.

One loud Whooooooo!

Two bunnies giggle.

"whooo-booo to you!"

One silver moon.

Two paws held tight.

Two brave bunnies.
One Halloween night.

To the family on Auburn Street.
And once again to Steve.—K. O. G.

For Kellie and Dillon—J. M.

Text copyright © 2008 by Kathryn O. Galbraith
Illustrations copyright © 2008 by Jeffrey M. Mack

All rights reserved. Published in the United States by Sandpiper, an imprint of
Houghton Mifflin Harcourt Publishing Company. Originally published in hardcover in the United States
by Harcourt Children's Books, an imprint of Houghton Mifflin Harcourt Publishing Company, 2008.

SANDPIPER and the SANDPIPER logo are trademarks of Houghton Mifflin Harcourt Publishing Company.

For information about permission to reproduce selections from this book, write to Permissions,
Houghton Mifflin Harcourt Publishing Company, 215 Park Avenue South, New York, New York 10003.

www.hmhbooks.com

The illustrations in this book were done in acrylic on watercolor paper.
The display type was set in House of Terror and Spookhouse.
The text type was set in Chaloops and Spookhouse.

The Library of Congress has cataloged the hardcover edition as follows:

Galbraith, Kathryn Osebold.
Boo, bunny! / Kathryn O. Galbraith; [illustrated by] Jeff Mack.
p. cm.
Summary: Two small bunnies face their fears while trick-or-treating on Halloween night.
[1. Fear—Fiction. 2. Rabbits—Fiction. 3. Halloween—Fiction. 4. Stories in rhyme.]
I. Mack, Jeff, ill. II. Title.
PZ8.3.G1216Boo 2008
[E]—dc22 2007021426

ISBN: 978-0-15-216246-7 hardcover
ISBN: 978-0-547-48031-2 paperback

Manufactured in China
LEO 10 9 8 7 6 5 4 3 2 1
4500218379